The Anatomical Hist

Nicola Ashb. ....

abuddhapress@yahoo.com

Alien Buddha Press 2022

©™®

Nicola Ashbrook 2022

ISBN: 9798841129752

The following is a work of fiction. Any similarities to actual people, places, or events, unless deliberately expressed otherwise by the author are purely coincidental.

For my dad, who inspired the espionage

Heart Failure, 2021

Violet Vee lies on her deathbed in the Cornflower Room of her local hospice. They'd given her the choice of here or Sunflower but this was an obvious choice, cornflowers taking Violet back to another life where flowers bloomed bright as the sky and she herself began her own blooming.

Violet is comfortable, a recent top-up of Morphine nicely softening the edges. She smiles, casts her still piercing eyes over her surroundings. Paul sits beside her, his wide hand hiding hers. She examines his face – poker-neutral. She isn't surprised, he's had plenty of practice at giving nothing away, but he catches her eye and she knows. She can read him as only a Russian native can truly read Cyrillic. After she's gone, people will wonder at his lack of grief – they'll collect in the church hall and comment how he's never shed a tear. Tut-tut, they will say, perhaps he never truly loved her. But only Violet knows about the secret chamber of his heart. Only Violet has the key. He squeezes her fingers and she squeezes back.

At the foot of the bed, grasping one another's hands are Karla, Yasmine and Francesca, Violet's daughters. She still thinks of them as her girls, but now she's ninety-three, Violet concedes her girls are getting old themselves. Francesca is even a grandmother! Violet snorts at the madness of it all, causing Karla, her youngest, to half-stand, half-dive towards her. Violet raises an enquiring eyebrow.

"I'm quite fine, darling," she says, "Don't get your knickers in a twist."

The door swings open and in peers Father Francis, the Catholic priest.

"Sure, Violet, I had a call from the sister – she says you requested the Last Rites?" he says in his Irish brogue. "Would now be convenient?"

Violet nods. She waits a beat.

"I'd like some privacy," she says, "If no one minds?"

Paul and the girls dutifully stand and make their way out of the private room.

"We don't think she has long now," Francesca says to the priest in a terrible attempt at a whisper, "Thank you so much for coming."

"Not at all, not at all," he says, winking at Violet as they file out.

He looks at the chair where Paul was seated as if his ghost remains, before moving to the other side of her bed and taking her other hand.

In the corridor, her girls wonder at the confessions their mother evidently wants to make on her deathbed. Paul stares at a fixed point out of the window.

"Do you think she has secrets?" they say.

"Mum? I doubt it."

"No, we know all there is to know about mum."

After a while, they file back in and resume their positions.

Violet thinks she should probably give them some motherly reassurance. But then again...

Violet looks at her daughters until she catches Yasmine's eye. She takes a croaky breath and allows her eyeballs to roll backwards.

Yasmine squeals.

"I think she's..."

"What?"

"Dead!"

There's a collective intake of breath. They all stand and lean towards her.

Violet slowly opens her eyes and grins. There's no rush, she thinks, no rush at all. Perhaps there's even time to remember it all one last time...

Broken Ulna, Fractured Radius, 1945

It's a dusty day in an unrelenting August when Violet decides she cannot stand another second of soul-crushing boredom. There has to be more to life than this. So she packs her red leather portmanteau with a small selection of essentials and simply walks out of the family home.

When she reflects on this moment later in life, she'll think only of the pain she must have inflicted on her parents. But, at the time, Violet is seventeen, assumes her parents are far too consumed in their own business to even notice she's gone, feels the world owes her something. Her teenage years have been stolen by The War. It's as though she has been paused since she was eleven, recently unpausing and finding she's a woman. A woman who is not suited to a life of cooking and sewing and keeping house.

So Violet places purposeful steps on the hot pavement and takes herself away.

She walks in a straight line until something blocks her path. This is where she's meant to go, she tells herself. The thing that blocks her path is an enormous white tent with a wooden sign above its door inscribed in a gaudy red and yellow with 'Spencer's Circus'. Without pause, Violet strides into the tent. On the central circular stage is an elephant topped with a fairy-like girl in a pink tutu. In front of the elephant, holding a curling whip is a tall, slim man with impossibly black hair.

"We open at seven tonight," he calls in an accent Violet associates with the aristocracy.

Instead of leaving, she strides closer.

"I'm here for a job," she says.

The man appraises her from his elevated position. A finger and thumb roll one edge of his handle bar moustache to a shiny point.

"Are you a circus artiste?" he says.

"Yes," Violet replies, the lie as easy as leaving home. She quickly scans the tent. "I do trapeze."

"How unusual!" Spencer says, "And absolutely fortuitous – we lost our trapeze girl just this morning."

By the time Violet has met the whole crew, been fitted with a costume and caked in an obscene layer of make-up it is too late to practise before the evening show. Gamely, and without fear, Violet climbs the rigging to the waiting trapeze. She holds tight, lets her feet leave solid footing. She flies!

This, this is better than darning socks.

It is only when she brazenly tries to hang from her feet, letting go with her hands, that Spencer sees this flame-haired beauty is not a trapeze artist at all. By the time she lands in a crumpled heap beside his best stilt-walker, Spencer is sure. But still, Spencer is awed. He doesn't meet many with the bottle of Violet Vee – to stride into his tent and onto the trapeze without so much as having visited a circus before (an admission she makes later). She may not be an artiste yet but, by gum, she could be. And perhaps, he cogitates, so much more even than that...

Labyrinthitis, 1953

Violet has been a cloistered nun for fourteen (long) days yet already she harbours some regrets.

It had seemed a good idea after leaving the circus to do something quieter – after all it was the cacophonic din which led to her resignation. At the beginning, she had enthusiastically ridden the noisy, swelling wave of adulation which accompanied every matinee and every evening show, easily believing the applause was hers alone. She thrived on the roar of the lion and the trumpet of the elephant, the growing crescendo of cymbals, the shrieks of children, the vibration of the drum roll. The circus sounds pulsated inside of her, like a second heartbeat, as natural and necessary as her vital organs.

That is until the day she climbed the rigging and the stage suddenly looked twice as far away as it should have and Violet faltered. Violet never faltered. It wasn't in her nature and it didn't make sense why it was happening now. Violet, being Violet, overrode all concerns and leapt from her rung as usual. As she flew across the stage, the usual blur of lights seemed brighter and harder to bear, the noise throbbed in her skull and an ominous nausea swirled through her stomach. Later,

17

Spencer said she turned the shade of a golden delicious before unceremoniously covering the stage and several other performers in a perfect arc of vomit.

The doctor came, diagnosing an inner ear disorder for which he prescribed bedrest and medication. Violet recovered, as he said she would, but the trapeze was never the same. The noise remained cacophonous, the lights too dazzling, the trapeze too high. So Violet, reluctantly, heartbroken to leave her circus family, tendered her resignation.

And now, after considering a range of quieter career opportunities, Violet, always drawn to extremes, finds herself here, at quite the opposite end of the noise spectrum, theoretically living a life of silent contemplation. But where she should be settling into the silence, her larynx itches for use. Where she has promised poverty, where she should be at one with her Habit, she isn't. She dreams instead of fishnet tights and tutus and slick leotards. She dreams of make-up and hairspray. She dreams of vertiginous heights no longer her own. She dreams of applause, of laughter, of jaunty calliope waltzes. She dreams, already, of creating cacophony in the silence.

Ruptured Hymen, 1953

Increasingly, Violet feels claustrophobic at the convent. She tries to concentrate on her prayers, she really does, but her brain is skittish, refusing to be focused on appropriate subjects of contemplation. Increasingly, she attends confession. Violet allows herself to believe this is because she has committed herself to God and must cleanse herself of sin in order to better serve him. She ignores the giddy part of herself which enjoys the sound of Father Francis' mellifluous voice lilting through the grate. She pretends the sound does not in fact cause an unusual flutter between her legs.

She pretends she does not think about his voice whispering quotes from Genesis close to her ears every night when she tries to sleep. And then, she thinks, perhaps this is reason enough to attend confession again.

She wonders just how honest she should be in confessing her sins to Father.

This tumult of thoughts tumbling through her brain, Violet sits on the cold varnished pew in the confessional. She can hear Father Francis – a much more youthful man than his title suggests, more youthful she

19

suspects even than herself – entering his half of the booth. He slides the wooden cover away from the grate, slowly, slower than necessary. Violet sees his fingers grazing the mesh. She takes an involuntary ingressive breath.

"Bless me Father, for I have sinned..." she begins.

"Sister Violet," he replies, "it seems you've had a very sinful week." Violet can hear his lop-sided (plush-lipped, kissable) grin shaping the edges of his words.

Violet's response is an indecipherable stammer.

Gently, so gently, Father Francis says, "Perhaps you're visiting so often because you're finding it hard to say what you really want to..."

Violet bites her lip. She shakes her head.

"I shouldn't be here, Father," she manages, "I can't keep my vows."

She doesn't stop to listen for a response. She's already pulling her Habit over her head, throwing it into a heap on the bench. She runs from the confessional wearing only her under-slip, pushing through the side door out into the churchyard, past the graves, the gate, away from

20

the church, the convent, the catechism. Violet runs until she doubles over in a cornfield, out of breath but free.

When Father Francis sits down beside her a few minutes later, there is no need for words. He grins that lop-sided grin before gently, slowly, lowering her onto the cornflowers.

Amenorrhea, 1953

It is eight weeks since Violet last bled. Initially she didn't notice but now she's filled with a deep dread that something is seriously wrong. The doctor doesn't seem too perturbed.

"The most common cause of Amenorrhea is pregnancy, Violet, could that be a possibility?"

Although now twenty-five, Violet is innocent to the more complex workings of the reproductive system. Sex education had barely featured in the curriculum of her all-girls school and despite recently experiencing certain urges, Violet had not hitherto associated them with pregnancy.

The doctor conducts some tests and announces her Amenorrhea is indeed due to being with child. Well, so be it, Violet thinks, Amen to that. Amen indeed.

That evening, Violet sits with a cup of tea in the motel in which she has managed to blag a room, pondering her next move. She's homeless, jobless, shortly to become a mother. She concludes this won't do. She considers going home but having been gone eight years it doesn't seem wise to suddenly re-appear in this state.

So Violet calls the only other person she trusts: Spencer.

"Don't fret, my darling," he says, after listening to her predicament, "I've been hoping you'd call. I've a solution which could solve both of our problems."

There'd be certain paperwork, he explained – Official Secrets Act and whatnot – but all Violet would need to do would be to let short-term tenants into a boarding house. She'd keep watch on proceedings, be his eyes and ears. The whole top floor would be her quarters. The pay would be handsome.

"Okay," Violet says, as though she has agreed to walk someone's dog, not become complicit in the activities of the security services. And so it is that Violet and her Amenorrhea caused by pregnancy move into Sunny Lane Boarding House.

"Amen," she says when she sees it, "Amen indeed."

Frozen Shoulder, 1953

It is a sultry day in late September when Violet wakes unable to move her head to the right. A quick visit to the doctor reveals a frozen shoulder. How ironic, Violet thinks, in this heat!

She takes the painkillers prescribed and returns a little wonkily to Sunny Lane. Waiting for her are the papers of her next tenant, no doubt delivered by one of Spencer's lackeys. He never visits himself – if they meet it is always elsewhere – but he ensures she knows everything about her tenants.

This file reveals a photograph of a handsome, blue-eyed man, with broad defined cheekbones, a faint dusting of stubble and a military grade buzz-cut. Russian, Violet guesses. Indeed, the file names him as Nikolai Dmitriev, KGB and double-agent. He'll be one for the watching, Violet thinks.

When he arrives later that morning, he doesn't engage with Violet's chatty greeting. He gives barely more than a grunt. Violet shows him to his room then shrugs off his rudeness. How ironic to be given the cold shoulder while suffering from a frozen one! Violet grins at her own wit, before surpassing herself by noting that at the end of the day, it is The Cold War.

Nikolai ignores her the next day and the next. Violet keeps an eye on his comings and goings, watches him with her head still fixed at an awkward angle as he smokes in the yard.

At 10pm on the hottest day, there's a knock at Violet's door. Despite only being in her slip, she answers it. Nikolai comes in without speaking. He closes the door behind him. Despite his background, Violet, being Violet, is not fearful. She looks him directly in the eye. He extends an arm to her left shoulder. He applies pressure. Violet doesn't break eye contact. He moves his bear-like hand to another spot and presses again. He has pressed in four places when Violet feels an over-whelming relief. She can move her head!

Something shifts in the humidity. Nikolai steps closer. He doesn't break eye contact. Neither does Violet. She can smell his cologne and smoke.

Nikolai pushes the strap of Violet's silk slip off her left shoulder. She doesn't flinch. With a slight raising of his eyebrows, Nikolai pushes the other strap from her other shoulder. The whole slip falls to the ground.

25

Violet doesn't break eye contact. She makes no attempt to cover herself.

It is Nikolai who lowers his eyes. It is Violet who reaches for his hand, it is Violet who skims it across her left breast. It is Violet who closes the gap.

How ironic, Violet thinks later, for the Cold War to be so incredibly hot.

Hypertension, 1953

It is not ideal to have pissed off the KGB. Not ideal at all.

Violet paces the living room. It has been quite a shock to discover that Nikolai is in fact married to the daughter of an extremely senior and influential KGB member and to discover, therefore, that she herself is now an adulterer and enemy of the Communist Regime. It's quite a feat to have achieved overnight.

Still, Violet reasons, absentmindedly rubbing circles on her just about still flat belly, we all have our secrets.

For an emotionless man of very few words, Nikolai seemed worryingly rattled when he confessed all earlier on.

As Violet paces, she's aware of her heart beating faster than it should, of a throbbing in her temple. Violet, being Violet, is not concerned with whether Nikolai is suitable life-partner material or whether it's wise to risk everything for him. She is merely concerned with preventing an assassin from darkening the door of Sunny Lane Boarding House. It seems a reasonable enough concern.

She calls Spencer. They meet at the third picnic bench from the duck pond at the local park.

By the end of the week, Nikolai Dmitriev is Paul Vee, with papers to prove it and he and Violet are two hundred miles away, settling into their new maisonette above Charming post office. They'll run the post office, which will also act as an information exchange for Spencer. Paul has ensured his ongoing protection by sharing a hitherto unknown Soviet plot to target London with a nuclear warhead. They all agree he can never return to Russia.

Paul is wearing a hat while his hair re-grows and spectacles which make Violet want him to give her a good telling off. He hasn't shaved in days, a dark beard now curling along his jawline. His black ribbed sweater and jeans have been replaced with a collared shirt, waistcoat and tailored trousers, all of which accentuate his muscular physique.

Violet's heart beats a little faster whenever she sees him and the throbbing in her temple has been replaced by a relentless throbbing elsewhere. It is not so bad, she thinks climbing into bed beside Paul, to have provoked the KGB after all.

Contracting Uterus, 1954

Paul is a gentleman. He's a gentleman when Violet reveals she's pregnant mere weeks after they meet. He's a gentleman in never questioning the dates, even when the baby arrives at least six weeks premature weighing a whopping nine pounds.

He's a gentleman when it comes to running the post office and making the meals (though cabbage features more often that Violet would like) and he's a gentleman on the day Violet gives birth, staying squarely at the head end.

He's a gentleman for mopping Violet's brow with a cold flannel and ignoring her colourful exclamations about fucking men, and a gentleman for telling her she looks beautiful afterwards, even though she has vomited and a smear of blood has somehow become encrusted on her cheekbone.

He's a gentleman for holding her when she cries from exhaustion in the middle of the night, saying she can't do this, can they just give the baby back and he says *you are tougher than KGB Violet Vee, you can do anything, but maybe I can hold the baby for a bit and you can sleep.*

He's a gentleman for not even asking her for sex until she practically rips his clothes off six weeks after giving birth and then, without any sort of prompt, tells her it's just as good as before, if not better.

Paul is definitely a gentleman. He's a gentleman through his measured use of words – never many but always good ones. He's a gentleman for the things he doesn't say, as well as the things he does.

He's a gentleman, he feels, in particular, for never mentioning the other baby – Ilya - the baby he had to leave behind.

Appendicitis, 1956

Violet is pushing Francesca on the swing with one hand and rocking baby Yasmine's pram with the other, when she is overcome by a stabbing pain in her stomach. She tries to straighten up but the pain cuts her in two. She yelps once, then crumples to the ground.

When Violet wakes up, she's lying under starched hospital sheets minus her appendix. According to Paul, who is clutching her hand, the girls are safe with Mrs Hazel from next door and Violet's life was saved by Fenton, the local vet, who albeit more specialist in cats and dogs does know an appendicitis when he sees one.

"Did he spay me while he was at it?" Violet asks, slurring slightly.

Paul laughs. Then, serious, "Violet, you know he just brought you in – an actual surgeon removed the appendix?"

"Good," Violet replies, "Because they love those awful rectal thermometers don't they?" before falling immediately back to sleep.

31

When Violet wakes again later, the ward is dim but she can see a priest standing beside the bed.

"Am I dead?" she asks.

"Not at all," he says, but as soon as he speaks Violet thinks she must be. How else could she be hearing that voice?

Father Francis sits down.

"Of all the patients, in all the wards…" he begins. He's stricken, Violet sees now, to meet her again. To see her like this.

"Violet," he says, "that day, in the cornfield, I think about it a lot…"

"Me too," she says, "all the time."

"I shouldn't have…"

"No."

"I never have…"

"Again?"

"No. Never before or since. I made a vow…"

"I know," Violet says, "I know. So did I."

She opens her hand, beckons with a finger until Father Francis slowly, gently, places his hand in hers.

Itchy Feet, 1963

Violet takes her youngest daughter, Karla, to school for the first time. Karla runs in without a backward glance, happy to be where her sisters are at last. Violet waves and begins her walk home.

She could go and help Paul in the post office but he has employees now and doesn't really need her to. Plus, there's something about having survived the pre-school years that makes her want to celebrate.

Violet walks past home and continues towards town. As she walks, she wonders what she'll do now, on a grander scale. How will she fill her days? How will she feel satisfaction? Challenge? She is not made for keeping house, of that much she's sure.

As Violet reaches a more built-up area, she actively diverts into the back alleys, searching, letting her instincts lead. Wherever they take her, that's where she's meant to be, she tells herself.

She stops at a non-descript blue door. There is nothing to suggest excitement behind it, yet Violet pushes and it opens. She climbs the dingy staircase. At the top are double glass doors, flanked by two women at least a decade younger than herself, wearing feathered headdresses and sequined bodices over tiny, flippy skirts.

"Welcome," they say in unison, holding open the doors.

Violet strides in. She's in a long room whose furthest wall is lined with a stage and neon lightbulbs spelling out 'Sapphire Iris'. She looks around. There is a mirrored bar, a dance floor and many round tables, some with people seated at them, mostly men. Violet proceeds through a smoky haze to the bar.

"I'm here to see the manager," she says.

"Dave!" the barmaid yells into the back, "Someone to see you."

Dave ambles out. He's squat and greasy of skin and hair.

"And who might you be?"

"I'm Violet, Violet Vee. I'm here for a job."

"Barmaid or hostess?"

Violet thinks of the feathered headdresses.

"Hostess."

"Right," he says, looking disdainfully at her demure knee-length shift dress.

"Any experience? Dancer?"

"Yes," Violet lies. How hard could it be?

Dave visibly dithers.

"Not sure we have an opening. We have to uphold certain, err, standards, you know? To draw in the clientele…"

Violet rolls her eyes. She reaches behind herself and unzips her dress. She wriggles it to the floor, revealing hot pink underwear and a body which does not suggest the carrying of three children. Violet raises an eyebrow.

"Sorry, yeah, sure. When can you start?" Dave practically aspirates on his own saliva.

Thinking that if he does expire, she'll leave him to it, Violet steps over her dress and walks purposefully around the bar.

"I assume costumes are this way?"

Black eye, 1965

In all the years Violet works at Sapphire Iris, there is only trouble on one occasion.

The usual crowd is eclectic – artists, agents (of the kind with whom Violet is already acquainted), businessmen, pop stars, writers. It is the kind of place everyone wants to frequent but no one talks about frequenting. It has a well-cultivated air of mystery which suits Violet arriving from the school run each morning dressed as Mother, working her shift and leaving again de-sequined, de-feathered, re-clothed as Mother at 2:30pm in order to pick up the girls. When they ask her over dinner what she has done all day, she says, "Oh nothing exciting, just chores my darlings."

Paul occasionally raises an eyebrow but he doesn't ask any questions. He has his secrets, she has hers.

In the club, there is a strict no touching policy and for all that Dave is greasy, he is strict in upholding it. Violet is paid to talk, to dance, to flirt, to titillate the eye. Never the hand. And, from day one, she is tipped handsomely to essentially be herself. So far, being herself has purchased Paul a Rolex, an enormous doll's house with all the accessories for the girls and a sapphire (of course) necklace for herself. Simply *being* Violet Vee is a lucrative business.

And all is well until the day Mr Dickens-Brent, the girls' head master, appears at midday (on a school day!) somewhat worse for the wear. He clocks Violet immediately. She gives him direct eye contact – she has nothing to be ashamed of – and offers him a drink. She brings him a Bloody Mary. As she bends to place it on the table, he slips a five pound note into her cleavage. Unimpressed, she ignores him. He grabs her wrist as she turns away and grips it tightly.

"I don't suppose the girls know their mother whores herself while they're at school, do they? I bet you wouldn't want them to... You'd be the talk of the playground if this got out. Can you imagine?" He sprays saliva as he spits out his words. "But we can keep it our little secret if you like? If you incentivise me, you catch my drift? Come on, good girl, show me to the private rooms."

Violet steps backwards, hard, so that her stiletto meets the top of his (ugly) shoe.

"Ow! You little bitch!" he yells. He grabs the back of her skirt as she tries to walk away. She keeps walking until it rips and dangles pathetically in his hand. "Prick tease!" he yells, "Get back here at once!"

He lunges for her and at least ten other men rise in unison, advancing as one. Fenton, the vet, gets there first.

"What did you call her?" he says, grabbing Mr Dickens-Brent (forever forth to be referred to by Violet as Mr Dick-for-brains) by the shoulder.

"A prick tease," he says again, too drunk to notice the shift in atmosphere.

"I don't think so," says Angus, an agent Violet knows well, pulling himself up to his full six feet-four.

"Mind your manners," says Dave, "In front of the ladies."

"Ladies?" Mr Dick-for-brains gives a sarcastic laugh, "She's a whore!"

At which point, a fracas breaks out and Violet is inadvertently elbowed in the eye. The brawl is short-lived, with ten men easily over-powering the interloper, who is frog-marched down the stairs and no doubt taught a further lesson at the bottom.

"What happened to your eye, Mama?" the girls ask at dinner.

"I slipped on a banana skin carrying the groceries and bashed it on a lamppost," Violet answers – a story the girls find hilarious and quickly add to family lore to be repeated through the decades in the context of how clumsy their funny little mother is.

The next day, Yasmine announces that Mr Dickens-Brent has left the school and isn't coming back.

"Is that so?" Violet says, fingering her sapphire necklace, "Is that so?"

Cirrhotic Liver? 1968 onwards

As the girls get older, especially during their teenage years, it becomes clear they are not going to employ the same purposeful blindness to Violet's comings and goings as Paul does. Having had charmed, stable childhoods, they have no concept of the need for secrecy or discretion. They are observant and direct in their questioning. They believe everything is as it seems – why would it be otherwise?

In order to be able to leave the house of an occasional evening and not answer myriad questions on the subject – she can hardly say she needs some private time with Father Francis or that she has a secret mission for Spencer or an extra shift at Sapphire Iris, can she? – Violet creates a fail-safe alibi. She tells them she's an alcoholic. She is not, and never has been, but a weekly 'meeting' provides excellent opportunities.

She tells them she's embarrassed and would rather they kept it a family matter. She tells them she attends a meeting two towns away to avoid being seen by someone they know, which buys her an extra forty-five minutes to an hour in 'travelling' time. The charade also buys her the admiration of her girls, who are impressed with her ownership of the problem and her pro-activity in courting recovery.

Violet, being Violet, feels no guilt at the deception, just pride in the genius of the solution. It is a solution she uses until the girls leave home and then re-imposes whenever they come to stay thereafter.

It is ironic then, when, a few years later, Violet starts to find half-consumed bottles of vodka hidden all over the maisonette. It is a masterful double-bluff – she can hardly call Paul out on it or suggest he seeks help when he has remained silent on her faux-alcoholism all this time, can she? Forever the double-agent it would seem.

But it rattles her, this loss of control from Paul who is usually their stabilising force. And Violet is never rattled. Nothing good will come of this, she sees now, nothing at all.

Déjà vu induced Insomnia, 1973

Violet returns from her shift at Sapphire Iris to prepare dinner. Apparently Francesca is bringing someone home. Violet is pleased about this – Francesca has always been so studious, so serious – it's about time she let her hair down a little. Violet is curious too – Francesca has told her little, except that it's a boy she met at university.

Yasmine, always wilder than her sisters, is out, no one is sure where. Karla, now in her last year of school, sits on the sofa completing her homework. Violet is making her trademark lasagne. She is not a natural cook but has managed to perfect a handful of dishes over the years. This is her best. Despite her short-comings, Violet tries hard to be the mother she thinks her children need. She places the lasagne in the oven and begins a salad.

When the front door opens, both Violet and Karla look towards it with curiosity. Francesca, in her best faux-posh voice introduces her friend as Ilya. Ilya greets Violet with a firm handshake and an accent she'd know anywhere: Russian.

Violet does a double-take and grips the counter. He has blue eyes, broad, defined cheekbones, a suggestion of stubble peppering his square jaw. Simultaneously, Violet thinks heatwave of 1953 and KGB. Neither makes sense.

She recovers enough to offer him a drink. While he and Francesca chat with Karla, Violet's mind races. Could he be an agent, here to dig into Paul? She supposes so, but… It is as though she's seen him before.

"What brings you to England?" Violet asks as they sit down to dinner.

"My studies," he says. Such familiarity in his economy of words! "Also, my father disappeared when I was a baby. My mother always thought he'd come to England. I'm not sure why. I don't know… It's silly but I think I'd hoped I'd find him here."

"I see," says Violet trying not choke at him using the word *here*, "And have you? Found him, I mean."

"No." He looks sad. Violet resists the temptation to comfort him. She thanks God Paul is not due back tonight. He's on a job for Spencer. She apologises for his absence, tells him, as they tell the girls, that he sometimes helps a friend with fruit and vegetable pick-up and delivery.

44

The lasagne is delicious. Conversation flows. Everyone enjoys their evening.

In bed, Violet asks herself if she should tell Paul. But if she did, it would raise the question of whether Francesca should really be dating her 'brother'. This is not a road Violet wants to go down, but she does feel better having ruled out the possibility of shared genes in her own mind, Francesca not exactly being Paul's and whatnot. Then, she wonders, does Paul know he has another child? Has he kept it from her all these years?

Violet tosses and turns until morning. It doesn't seem a plausible solution to always make sure Paul is out whenever Ilya visits but surely the two must never meet?

The problem is solved more quickly than anticipated by Francesca herself, who announces at breakfast that Ilya is returning to Russia to complete his studies and as handsome as he is, his looks are probably not sufficient to sustain their relationship across the whole of a continent.

45

Thank God, Violet thinks, thank heavens for that. Paul can keep his secrets and she can keep hers.

Broken Heart, 1980

It's autumn. The leaves are in full flamboyance. Violet spends a pleasant morning wandering around an art exhibition before having lunch with a friend. She goes home slowly, dancing around orange leaves floating down from the trees.

She arrives to see Suliman, Spencer's partner, perching on the wall outside of the post office. She's met Suliman several times over the years, but only ever alongside Spencer. She's very fond of him but seeing him here, alone, feels off. A strange shiver passes down her spine.

"Hi," she says, greeting him with a kiss, "To what do I owe this pleasure?"

"I think I'd better come in," he says, taking her hand and patting it.

Violet makes a pot of tea and they sit side by side on the sofa in the bay window, their backs to the small high street below.

"Violet," he says, "I'm so sorry but Spencer is gone."

"Where?" she asks, thinking his work has taken him to some far-flung destination.

Suliman's eyes cloud and tears spill down his cheeks.

"Gone."

Violet feels her heart compress as though someone has reached into her rib cage and grabbed it with their fist.

"Oh Sully," she says, pulling him to her, wrapping her arms around him. "How?"

"Something awful, Vi. A cancer maybe. They don't know. He had all these sores and the weight just fell off him. His breathing…" Suliman breaks down.

"Some friends have it too," he says when he recovers a little. "I think it's something awful targeting gay men. I can't explain it, but there were so many in the hospital Vi, in the same sorry state as our dear Spencer."

Violet is too shocked to cry but later, after Suliman has gone, she weeps and weeps. Spencer was her oldest friend. She's loved him for

48

thirty-five years like a reliable older brother. It's hard to imagine a world without him in it – he has always been there, having her back. Violet has lost people before but no one so close, no one so vital.

It will be days before she can get dressed. By the time she is ready to re-engage with life, all the trees will be naked, held brittle by a frigid and unforgiving winter.

And by then, Violet will have realised that if it is thirty-five years since she first met her beloved Spencer, it is also thirty-five years since she's been home. She doesn't even know if her parents are still living but if this doesn't make her find out, what will?

Urticaria, 1981

With Spencer gone, Violet and Paul must answer to a new representative of the security services – a Mrs. Helena O'Hunt. They meet her on a frosty February day in the back room of a dingy pub fifteen miles from the post office. She's a short woman, sturdy-looking but not so careless as to be fat. Her grey hair is cut into a regimented bob – all straight lines and symmetry – and her face centres on her small, puckered mouth, her cheeks sucked in and her eyebrows raised in disgust, as though she can permanently smell cat urine. Violet senses immediately that she and Helena will not be friends.

As soon as Helena begins to speak, skipping any pleasantries entirely, Violet begins to itch. First on her hands, then her arms and legs, and even on her stomach. It's very uncomfortable.

Helena begins by telling them all the ways in which Spencer has failed to manage them correctly. She draws out a lengthy list of rules which must be adhered to henceforth. She tells them they should not be entertaining guests without a security check in their home, Paul should not be seen off travelling God-only-knows-where running errands for God-only-knows-who (but certainly not them), Violet should not *fraternise* with the people with whom they see her *fraternising,* the administration of the post office itself leaves much, *much* to be desired and could they not, for the actual love of God, file their paperwork correctly...

Violet tunes out. It's hard to concentrate without scratching her increasingly itchy body. She can feel herself wriggling in her seat. She tries to tune back in, wondering what Paul makes of all this. She snatches a sideways glance at him, while surreptitiously scratching the inside of her elbow, but his gaze is fixed on Helena and his face is expressionless.

When Helena's monologue has been going for what seems like half an hour but is probably only four minutes, Paul suddenly slams his palms hard onto the table and lets out an angry tirade in Russian. Violet sits to attention because Paul never loses his temper and never speaks Russian, not once in all the years they've been together.

"Paul, if you don't mind, remember your decorum. We are in a public place and you are *English!* Look, here, rule forty-five..." Helena hisses.

"My apologies Mrs Hunt," Paul says in his best received pronunciation, making the aitch harder and more like a 'k', "But if you would be so kind as to fuck right off with your ridiculous rules, I'd be most grateful."

Helena splutters, almost spitting her tonic water (no gin, too up tight) down herself.

"I beg your pardon? That is no way to speak to your commanding officer..."

"Apologies, Commanding Officer, but if you could shove your rules and your *role* and your expectations and your judgement up your tightly-wound arsehole we'd be much obliged. Wouldn't we Violet?"

"Yes!" Violet says, finding this unexpected display of carefully controlled machismo somewhat arousing.

"This insubordination is absolutely unacceptable! I shall have to remove all your security privileges; you are merely proving yourselves to be the loose cannons I thought you were. You will need to vacate the post office tout suite..."

"Don't worry love, you can shove that up your arse as well," Paul says back in his usual accent, standing and offering a hand to Violet who takes it and skips happily out with him.

"Are you ok?" he says to her when they get outside, "You seemed to be scratching at yourself in there like a dog with fleas."

"I think I was allergic to her," Violet replies. "The itching is stopping already." At which they both dissolve into hysterics. It takes quite some time for them to re-gain control.

In the car on the way home, Violet says, "I can't lie Paul, that display was sexy as hell. And she had it coming, she really was a c… Anyway, whatever she was, what do we do now?"

"Yeah, I'm sorry, it wasn't the plan to come out homeless and jobless…"

"I know. You did the right thing, neither of us could be beholden to her. But we'll have to leave the post office sharpish I think…"

"Try not worry, my love, we have plenty of money put away. We'll easily buy our own place. We can do whatever we want – fresh start."

"Ok," Violet says, as easily as agreeing to a free meal out. "What have you always wanted to do?"

"I've always fancied my own motorbike shop. What about you?"

"I've always wanted to live at the seaside."

And as easily as that, Violet and Paul move on, leaving all sources of irritation behind them.

Broken Leg? 1981

Violet has decorated the new house and helped Paul choose his new retail space and explored every shop and cafe in the seaside town they've recently moved to. It is now September and she's bored. Once more, her itchy feet take her through the backstreets. Once more she promises herself they'll take her wherever she needs to go.

Violet stops beside a large poster, housed inside an olive-coloured wooden frame. On it is the word 'AUDITIONS' in a hot pink font, reminiscent of the hot pink underwear which snagged her previous job. Violet reads. Apparently she is outside of an art house theatre and they are planning to put on a play called 'Pizzazz'. Auditions are this afternoon.

Violet strides in, straight into the auditorium where hopefuls are traipsing onto the stage one by one to perform in front of a judging panel. She stands at the back and observes. A young girl with dyed blue hair and heavily kohl-lined eyes performs a dramatic death scene. "Next!" yells the central member of the three-strong panel, evidently a hard-to-please older lady.

A tall man tries his luck but he's so deadpan and expressionless that Central Panel Lady, barely controlling her temper, yells at him to stop wasting her time.

The next hopeful, a girl of thirty or so, performs her whole scene without interruption. Promising, Violet thinks. Central Panel Lady then pipes up: "The role we'd consider for you involves nudity. Is that something you could manage?" The girl stammers and looks uncomfortable but says she thinks she could. "Go ahead," CPL says. The girl hops from foot to foot, twiddling with the bottom of her jumper, before bursting into tears and running from the stage.

Violet seizes the opportunity, striding forwards and up onto the stage.

"Name?" CPL calls.

"Violet, Violet Vee."

"Not on the list. Next!"

"I'm very comfortable with nudity," Violet says, not moving anywhere.

"That's what the last one said," CPL retorts, looking up to heaven.

"I'm a very experienced actress," Violet goes on, "You'd be lucky to have me."

"Got a cocky one here," CPL says to Left Panel Member, elbowing him.

"If you're so good, perform a monologue as if you're Margaret Thatcher talking about… err, I don't know… what should we have her talk about Daph?"

"How about the Soviet Union?" Right Panel Member chips in.

"And if you're so bloody comfortable with nudity, you might as well get your kit off as well," CPL adds.

Violet sees the panel sniggering and nudging one another. The bar is low; failure expected. I'll show them, Violet thinks, I'll wipe the bloody smirks off their smug little faces. Without skipping a beat, she begins acting like Margaret Thatcher talking aloud to herself in a bathroom, undressing herself and climbing into an imaginary bath. She keeps up a nuanced commentary on the state of the Soviet Union while she's at it, something which isn't difficult for her given Paul's close scrutiny of all the news bulletins on the subject. She ends, lying on the stage, one leg crossed over the other, barely hiding her modesty, waxing lyrical on the infrequent sightings of Brezhnev, speculating that perhaps his eyebrows, large as they are, may just have taken him hostage.

The panel is silent.

Applause breaks out amongst the remaining hopefuls. Violet stands, takes a bow and, full frontal, asks the panel if they'd like to give her any feedback. CPL is visibly stunned. Left Panel Member tries to recover himself.

"That was impressive," he manages, avoiding looking directly at Violet, "Wasn't it Pru? Daph?"

Slowly, CPL – Pru – takes to her feet. All her earlier malice has disappeared.

"Violet, my dear, I am very rarely wrong, but just now I was. You weren't being cocky. You *are* exceptional and if you'll accept my heartfelt apologies, we would indeed be lucky to have you."

And just like that, Violet finds herself a job.

Violet isn't sure she wants her girls to see her performing (particularly nude) so she tells them she's joined an am dram group as a hobby – that should deter them. She does tell Paul the truth though and before every show he always tells her to break a leg. On opening night, he's in the audience. And then because he enjoys her performance so much – Violet really does shine on stage, he feels – he comes once a week. And on those nights, Violet seems to shine just a little bit brighter still.

Phantom cramps, 1983

The small art house theatre has grown somewhat since Violet began her residency – tickets sell out every night and at the weekend they perform matinees too. The current play involves Violet playing a burlesque dancer, a role she has taken to with ease. She is particularly keen on the nipple tassels.

It's a Tuesday night in a cool April and Violet is getting ready as she always does. She has stayed in bed until 10am, been for a walk along the beach, drank a lot of tea and been to a yoga class. She's had fish and chips for dinner and is now affixing her tassels ready for the curtain call. As she sticks on the left one, she feels a sudden cramping in her abdomen. It's like a period pain but she's passed the menopause. It's a bit disconcerting – surely all that isn't going to happen again? Especially when she's going to be performing on stage in skimpy underwear. She tries to attach the right tassel and ignore the pain but it comes again. It's stronger this time, more reminiscent of giving birth.

The pain eases and Violet moves through to hair and make-up. A few minutes later, the pain comes again, making her grip the shelf in front of her and Yazz, the make-up girl, swear as Violet's eyeliner veers up her temple. The pains continue to come and go every three minutes or so.

"Are you having a baby Vi?" Yazz asks, "And if you aren't, which I kind of think you're not because I don't think there's space in that tiny stomach of yours for one, what on earth is happening to you?"

"Good God, no, I'm too old for all that! I had my babies years ago. In fact my eldest, Francesca, is due to give birth herself, any day now."

Violet takes a sharp intake of breath and Yazz clamps her hand to her mouth as they both have the same thought at the same time.

"Oh my God, Vi, do you think she's in labour now?"

There are ten minutes before the show starts but Violet runs outside (in full costume, hair and make-up, much to the shock of a passing dog-walker) to the nearest payphone. She calls Rob, Francesca's husband, but of course there's no answer – he's most likely at the hospital. She calls Paul, who hasn't heard anything but says he'll drive down just in case. She calls Yasmine, who tells her that yes, Francesca is indeed in labour, is she psychic?

"Kind of," Violet says, doubling-over with another spasm, "Kind of."

It is the most difficult show Violet has ever performed. As the curtain comes down, the pains suddenly ease.

In a hospital fifty miles away, Ashley Violet is placed on her mother's chest, making a cacophonous cry for such a small infant. Francesca, done with swearing at Rob for the sins of fucking men, stares down at her in awe. She strokes her downy head and thinks how she can't wait to show her to her own mother.

Sprained Ankle, 1990

"I have to go," Paul says over breakfast, apropos of nothing, one grey January morning.

"Where?" Violet asks, eating her muesli and barely glancing up from the newspaper.

"Home," he says. This gets her attention because she wonders whether all the vodka has finally pickled his brain.

"You are home."

"You know what I mean – Russia."

"Paul, you can't! Remember what Spencer said. It's far too risky."

"Darling, I have to. The regime is collapsing. It isn't the same now. I think this might be my only chance before things change again. Besides, I have my papers, don't I? I'm British. They'd have no reason to dig deeper."

Violet wants to press him. She wants to know why. She wants to know what he'll do there, who he will see. But she can't ask – that isn't their arrangement. Instead she says, "Will you come back?"

Paul stands and encircles her in his still muscular arms. He kisses the top of her head.

"I will always come back, you know that. I belong here with you. But I have to go, just this once. I need to."

Violet nods and leans her head against his arm.

On the day he goes, dense feathers of snow fall from the heavy, grey sky all day and all night. Violet cannot content herself, pacing around the house. She talks to Francesca who now has three girls of her own. She talks to Yasmine who has just had her first baby, a boy. She talks to Karla, who has declared herself a lesbian and shacked up with a butch-looking RSPCA officer. Violet doesn't disapprove per se – she did after all once spend a very enjoyable and enlightening afternoon with a fellow hostess from Sapphire Iris (Sapphic Iris that day) – she just doesn't understand why anyone's shoes need be so sensible or their clothes so shapeless.

She tells them all Paul has gone to London for business, then paces some more.

The next morning, in an act of rebellion against Karla's lover's fashion crimes, Violet dresses in her favourite outfit complete with heeled boots. It is not until her feet slide from under her the second they touch the pavement that Violet remembers the snow. And the incompatibility of it with her leather soles. Swearing, she looks at her ankle which is throbbing and double its usual size. It is all she can do to drag herself back into the house, through to the living room and to drag the boot from her foot.

Now she cannot pace, she is reduced to waiting. And hoping. Come back Paul, she thinks, please come back.

Labrynthitis relapse, 1991

Giddy with relief at Paul's return and apparent sobriety, Violet buys them a hot air balloon ride to celebrate. Initially it's romantic. They lean against the edge of the basket, his arm around her waist, peering down at all their favourite landmarks, trying to spot their house, their beach hut, the theatre. There's a gust of wind and the basket wobbles. Suddenly, everything looks twice as far away as it did. Suddenly the wind is too loud and the sun too bright. Violet feels like she's on a trapeze.

"Paul," she says, "I feel..." She doesn't get to the end of the sentence. Paul says later he didn't know a hot air balloon was able to descend so quickly.

At home, he carries her to the sofa. She waits for the doctor then she waits for the medication to work. Paul closes the curtains and puts the TV on quietly for her, even though she can't bear to look at it.

Violet drifts in and out of sleep.

She wakes to a breaking news story: Freddie Mercury is dying of something called AIDS. The newsreader is at a specialist hospital, finding out about this dreadful disease. Violet listens carefully. At the end, a realisation hits her: this is what took Spencer. Still nauseous and unable to get off the sofa, Violet feels impotent. She has never before been so desperate to *do* something.

A few days later, when she has recovered, she walks to the local GUM clinic. She walks straight to the counter and demands the largest box of condoms they have.

"Why, you planning on having a heavy weekend?" the receptionist deadpans.

"Hilarious. No, they aren't for me. I need to stop AIDS."

"By yourself?"

Violet rolls her eyes. "Someone has to do something."

"Well, good luck with that love, we offer all sorts of educational courses but hardly anyone attends."

By the end of the day, every bar and club in the town has a basket of free condoms in its bathroom. By the end of the week, Violet has arranged three school visits, attended the local gay club to talk to people and personally hand out condoms, and she's persuaded Pru at the theatre to give all the proceeds of one Saturday night performance per month to The Terence Higgins Trust.

Violet never goes in another hot air balloon as long as she lives, but on Aids Awareness Day, she commissions one with Spencer's face on it. She pays the pilot to throw condoms from it. Because if there's one thing Violet is passionate about, it's sex. And though love can make you dizzy, it should never, ever kill you.

Millennium Bug, 1999/2000

Although Violet finds it hard to believe that a new century is turning and that she's living to see it, she also thinks all the fuss about a millennium bug switching everything off at midnight is nonsense. The world has not been through all it's been through for a weird tech glitch to end everything now. Every time it is mentioned on TV, Violet switches channels. She has stopped reading the newspaper. She has even checked with Father Francis – in case he has insider information from God – so she's quite convinced it will be a New Year like every other.

She and Paul have hosted a big family Christmas. All the girls and their partners came and the six children they have between them – Francesca's three girls (Ashley is sixteen already!), Yasmine's boy and girl and the most recent addition, Karla and Jodie's son, Toby (best use of a turkey-baster to date). Violet has enjoyed every minute of it. She loves the chaos of the children, the noise, even the mess. It makes her feel more alive. She has made sure to spend one on one time with each of her grandchildren and to lead all of them slightly astray, but not so much as their mothers will notice. She also organised raucous games to keep them all entertained at once – musical chairs, apple bobbing, sardines. Nobody wanted to go home.

Paul says he's a bit tired in the aftermath and would like a quiet night in, but Violet isn't. Violet, being Violet, is ready for an almighty New Year's party. Through her work with AIDS charities, she has become friends with the guys who run the local gay club, Peachy. They are putting on a feather and sequins night and Violet is desperate to show them the best way to work that theme (she still has her Sapphire Iris outfit. It still fits.).

But on New Year's Eve morning, Violet wakes feeling strange. She wonders if it might be another labrynthitis attack and takes her meds. But Paul doesn't feel right either. He has the constitution of a well pickled ox and is never ill, so this is ominous. After breakfast, Violet finds she cannot get off the toilet. Neither can Paul. Thankfully, they have more than one bathroom. By lunch time, they are both vomiting.

When they manage to drag themselves to the living room later, both dragging a bucket with them, Violet drily quips, "I guess it's that Millennium Bug."

"I thought you didn't believe in that," Paul groans.

"I guess I was wrong."

Yasmine calls later. Their New Year's is ruined because Max is vomiting. So is Toby, Karla and Jodie, so are two of Francesca's brood.

"Bloody children," Paul says, "Grimey little buggers. And they do love to share."

"Generous, aren't they?"

Violet doesn't mind too much. Her stomach has settled by evening and there's something romantic about the two of them curled up under blankets together, watching another year in.

It's disappointing about the sequins and feathers though. But when Ant and Jord hear what's happened, they decide to hold another event in honour of Violet – because they adore her and want to thank her for her tireless campaigning but also to see if she really can give Kylie the run for her money she says she can.

She tells Paul she's working, going out dressed in a long trench. At Peachy, she makes her entrance on stage, appearing from behind two hot pink ostrich feathers to woops and cheers. She allows herself to be carried by two oily, topless young men to a podium where she proves,

71

without a shadow of a doubt that even at forty years her senior, she can indeed give Kylie a serious run for her money.

Jet lag, 2008

As Violet has got older, she has become acutely aware of the differential between her actual age and the age she feels inside. It beggars belief that she's about to turn eighty. Paul and the girls and the grandkids keep asking her how she'd like to celebrate but it's difficult to decide what would satisfy her. She is not the small gathering and tasteful cake type.

Then, one Thursday evening, driving back from Father Francis', the perfect solution reveals itself to her. She'd like to go around the world.

Violet has never left England. She probably would have done had it not been for Paul's dubious paperwork situation making it too risky. But now that he's been back and to Russia, she assumes his passport must pass muster. And she has been so busy having fun where she is. But suddenly, she wonders what else is out there. Those pesky itchy feet of hers suddenly itch again.

She tells Paul as soon as she gets home and he says, "Okay," as though he's agreeing to watch the omnibus of Eastenders. They visit the travel agent the very next day, planning a comprehensive trip which will take them to Rio, Cuba, Vegas, Thailand, Dubai, South Africa, Marrakech, Italy and Spain. They'll travel for the most-part of a year. They won't visit Russia, obviously. It costs a fortune but Paul points out it's mostly paid for by MI5 so it'd probably be rude not to.

Violet's only concern is whether an aeroplane is basically a trapeze, only higher, and therefore whether she'll be plagued by dizziness and nausea on all the flights but the doctor is a doll and gives her a bottle of magic pills which she promises will prevent anything untoward. She doesn't mention they will also make Violet sleep like she's comatose and/or talk a lot of nonsense. And occasionally sing. But those things don't concern Violet (just everyone else on the plane.)

The whole family come to the airport to wave them off. The girls are a little tearful and Violet is sure this is because they think she's far too old for such endeavours and will surely pop her clogs en route, the daft things. She may be eighty, but her heart is twenty-five. She'll show them, she thinks, clutching her new smart phone – the carnival is on when they're in Rio and she's come prepared with an outfit…

Laryngitis, 2014

Violet wakes one promising spring morning without any voice. Initially she puts it down to over-zealous singing at the recent concert she attended but then her temperature flares. The doctor prescribes anti-biotics and voice rest. The voice rest is a challenge for Violet and somewhat of a blessing for Paul he says, winking.

Violet finds scraps of paper and begins to communicate with Paul through the medium of witty notes, like *pretend I'm whispering sweet nothings* or **shouting so you'll hear me* can you put the bins out?*

It turns out Violet is verbose in note-writing so soon it gets harder to find a scrap of paper. She rummages in a drawer in the study to find more. She has never been one for studying, unless you count studying body language, men or fashion, so the 'study' is actually a room used mainly by Paul to keep on top of the household paperwork. He has applied the same filing system that irked Mrs Helena O'Hunt so much – haphazard, unorthodox, only decipherable to him. Violet opens a drawer at random and pulls out the first piece of paper she finds. It's a telephone bill. The printing is only on one side so she takes it to write on the back. Before she does so, something makes her cast her eye down the lines of print.

Almost all of the numbers are her calling the girls, which makes sense because Paul rarely uses the phone and in normal circumstances, Violet talks to one of the girls, or grandchildren, at least once a day. But one number is different. It's international. Someone has rung it once per week for the month displayed on the page. She goes back to the drawer. Someone has made the same call once per week for the previous five phone bills. They have been making the same call for potentially much longer than that but Paul's filing system… Violet has no idea where the rest of the bills could be.

Violet fetches her smart phone. She Googles the international dialling code. She knows the answer before it flashes up: Russia.

Violet sits quietly on the desk chair, pondering. Perhaps Paul re-connected with his wife when he visited Russia. Perhaps he's been calling her. Perhaps he met someone else. But Violet's instincts say no. She knows he loves only her and she trusts her instincts. She thinks heatwave of 1953, she thinks KGB, she thinks lasagne. She thinks *he's found him.* And she thinks *I'm glad.* It's only right a father should know his son.

She tucks the phone bills back into the drawer and pulls out an electricity statement instead. She writes *I love you. Lasagne for tea?*

Arthritic Hip, 2018

Although Violet has a few aches and pains these days, particularly in her right hip, she finds it best to ignore them. The doctor mentions something about a hip operation but Violet isn't interested in that nonsense. She swims in the sea every day and that does the trick. The same doctor suggests that being as though she is now weeks from her ninetieth birthday, perhaps it would be wise for her to slow down a little. She tells him she'll be pretty bloody slow when she's dead so she doesn't fucking think she will be slowing down any time soon, if ever, thank you very much. He asks her not to verbally abuse him and she writes him a prescription for a sense of humour and some balls. Then she gets black-listed from the surgery – apparently patients should never, without exception, touch the prescribing pad.

Returning home, Violet feels inspired to organise the most un-ninetieth ninetieth birthday party possible, for fun, but also to spite them all. She rings Ant and Jord from Peachy. They don't run the club any more but they do own an events planning business normally reserved for the rich and famous. To them, Violet Vee is an icon and they would be honoured to organise whatever the hell she wants.

And they do.

Violet wears a violet-coloured, figure-hugging, sequined dress with a thigh-high split. She has a feather headpiece made to match. She wears silver strappy sandals with a three instead of four inch heel – the only concession she is willing to make to her age.

The party is held in the local ballroom, which has been festooned by Ant and Jord with violet balloons, orchids, hot pink ostrich feathers and young topless, oiled men serving canapes and drinks. There is a chocolate fountain, photo booth, fire-eaters and stilt-walkers. When everyone is seated for dinner, a burlesque show takes place moving between the tables. Francesca, Yasmine and Karla seem a little shocked by it all but Violet is too old to hold back. The grandchildren, all in their twenties and thirties now, and used to being let in on secrets Violet keeps from their mothers, have brought their friends, knowing this will be quite the event. Violet is pleased there are young people here – they make it feel younger and more vibrant.

Everyone she knows has been invited – the agents they used to work with, girls she knew from Sapphire Iris, Dave, Fenton and some of the other locals they knew from their time at the post office, the theatre crew and a huge portion of the local gay community. The atmosphere is raucous. There are wildly varying interpretations of the 'wear your favourite outfit theme', with more than one PVC thong and pair of chaps spotted.

After dinner, Ant and Jord have used their connections to snag a famous boy band who play their own songs and covers of all Violet's favourite songs too. The tables are pushed to the sides and everybody piles onto the dance floor. Violet ignores her hip and dances for hours, only stopping to cut her enormous sparkly birthday cake. She dips and sways around the floor, making sure to dance with every guest in turn.

At 1am, Ant and Jord have organised a fireworks display over the sea, so all the guests traipse out onto the beach, wrapped in an assortment of jackets and blankets. Paul squeezes Violet to him as they stare at the sky, mesmerised by the jewel-like colours raining down on them.

"How are you?" he says when it's finished. "Have you enjoyed it?"

"It's been amazing," she says, "All I hoped and more. Have you?"

"Of course," he says, kissing her. "It's been perfect."

"I have to admit my hip is a little sore though."

Paul sees that unmistakable glint in her eye.

"It's going to be cold," he says.

"I know, that's the point," she says, pulling him. He laughs and runs with her, right into the sea, until she's gliding along like a sequined mermaid.

Heart Failure, 2021

Violet lies on her deathbed in the Cornflower Room of her local hospice.

Violet is comfortable, a recent top-up of Morphine nicely softening the edges. She smiles, casts her still piercing eyes over her surroundings. Paul sits beside her, his wide hand hiding hers. He squeezes her fingers and she squeezes back.

At the foot of the bed, grasping one another's hands are Karla, Yasmine and Francesca. All the grandchildren have visited in the last week and Ashley brought her daughter, Nancy Violet, Violet's precious great-grandchild.

Father Francis has visited and Violet has said all the things she needs to say. She has enjoyed one last kiss of that lop-sided grin.

It's been blissful re-living it all one last time, nearly as good as living it. Violet is satisfied she has squeezed every last drop of joy from life. She has made the most of every second. She has probably lived at least three lives in one lifetime. She feels surrounded by love, she *is* surrounded by love.

She hears Spencer calling.

Violet, being Violet, is not fearful. She closes her eyes and lets go of solid footing.

She flies.

Nicola Ashbrook is also author of Mae in Quinquennia, another novella-in-flash available through Selcouth Station, and The Art of Escapology, a flash fiction collection from Bearded Badger Press.

Long before she started to write, she worked as a speech and language therapist for children and still does.

She lives in Cheshire, England with her husband, boys, cats and an overly friendly Boston Terrier. When she isn't writing a novel, she can usually be found in the garden or putting together a colourful outfit.

www.nicolalostinnarration.weebly.com

@NicolaAWrites Twitter & Insta

.

Printed in Great Britain
by Amazon

85251315R00051